A Note from Michelle about the Super-Duper Sleepover Party

Hi. I'm Michelle Tanner. I'm eight years old. My big sister Stephanie is so lucky! She had a sleepover party. She invited a whole bunch of her friends. Now I want to have a sleepover party, too. And I want all my friends to come. Even though lots of people already live in my house.

There's me and my dad. Then there are my two older sisters, D.J. and Stephanie. But that's not all.

My mom died when I was little. So my uncle Jesse moved in to help Dad take care of us. So did Joey Gladstone. He's my dad's friend from college. It's almost like having three dads. But that's still not all!

First Uncle Jesse got married to Becky Donaldson. Then they had twin boys, Nicky and Alex. They're three years old now. And they're so cute.

That's nine people. And our dog, Comet, makes ten. Sure, it gets kind of crazy sometimes. But I wouldn't change it for anything. It's so much fun to live in a full house!

FULL HOUSE™: MICHELLE novels

The Great Pet Project
The Super-Duper Sleepover Party

Available from MINSTREL Books

FULL HOUSE™
Michelle

The Super-Duper Sleepover Party

Megan Stine

A Parachute Press Book

A MINSTREL® BOOK

PUBLISHED BY POCKET BOOKS

New York   London   Toronto   Sydney   Tokyo   Singapore

A MINSTREL PAPERBACK *Original*

A Minstrel Book published by
POCKET BOOKS, a division of Simon & Schuster Inc.
1230 Avenue of the Americas, New York, NY 10020

A Parachute Press Book
Copyright © 1995 by Warner Bros. Television

FULL HOUSE, characters, names and all related indicia
are trademarks of Warner Bros. Television © 1995.

ISBN: 0-671-51906-9

First Minstrel Books printing February 1995

10 9 8 7 6 5 4 3 2

A MINSTREL BOOK and colophon are registered trademarks of
Simon & Schuster Inc.

Printed in the U.S.A.

The Super-Duper
Sleepover Party

Chapter

1

♥ "Michelle! For the last time—please go away!" Stephanie Tanner said.

Eight-year-old Michelle Tanner looked around the living room. All of Stephanie's seventh-grade friends were having fun. Some were dancing and talking. Others were hunting for party prizes. Sleeping bags and pillows were everywhere.

Michelle put her hands on her hips. "No fair," she said to her big sister. "Why do

I have to leave? Just because you're having a slumber party?"

"No," Stephanie said. "Just because you're *ruining* my party."

"I am not," Michelle said. "I'm only trying to join in the treasure hunt game."

"Yes, but there is one big problem," Stephanie said. "You know where all the prizes are. You were here this afternoon when Dad and D.J. hid them for me!"

"So what?" Michelle asked.

"So you've already 'found' four of the treasures," Stephanie complained. "Now give them back—and go away."

Michelle twisted her mouth into a pout. But she reached into her pockets anyway. She pulled out the party prizes: two packs of gum, one polka-dot headband, and a pencil with a troll on top.

"Here," Michelle said. "Take your silly treasures. But you'll be sorry. I'm going to have a party of my own. And then I won't let *you* come."

"I'll risk it," Stephanie said. "Now go."

Michelle stood staring at the party for a minute more. She hated to leave.

"Psst—Michelle. In here," a voice called.

Michelle looked toward the kitchen door. Her uncle Jesse was standing there. He motioned to her.

"In here," Uncle Jesse repeated. "Popcorn. Come quick!"

Michelle giggled. Uncle Jesse was funny. He and his wife Becky lived upstairs in the attic. They had two small boys—twins named Alex and Nicky.

But the four of them were only part of the big family living in the Tanner house. There was Michelle, of course. And her two older sisters, Stephanie and D.J. And Michelle's dad, Danny Tanner.

That made eight.

Then there was Joey Gladstone. He was a friend of Danny's. Joey had moved into the house to help out when Michelle's mother died. That was a long time ago. Now he was just like part of the family.

That made nine. Nine people living in Michelle's house all together. Michelle liked to say you could just barely count them on your fingers. If you counted Comet, the dog, then all ten fingers were used up.

Uncle Jesse called to Michelle. "The popcorn is ready. Hurry! You can get the buttery pieces before anyone else!"

Michelle hurried into the kitchen. Uncle Jesse and her dad were making popcorn for Stephanie's party. But Danny looked worried.

"Popcorn is so messy," Danny said.

"Are you sure Stephanie's friends can eat that much?"

"Lighten up," Uncle Jesse said. "It's just a bowl of popcorn."

"I know, but popcorn is one of the messiest foods in the world," Danny said. "It jumps out of the bowl all by itself. Haven't you ever noticed that? It will get all over the rug."

"It does not," Jesse said. "It only gets on the rug when you toss it up in the air and try to catch it in your mouth."

"That sounds like fun!" Michelle said.

Danny rolled his eyes. "Don't give her any ideas," he said to Jesse.

"Daddy, can I have a sleepover party?" Michelle asked.

"Not tonight, honey," Danny said. "Your sister and her friends are making enough of a mess."

"I don't mean *tonight*," Michelle said.

She put her hands on her hips. "I mean for my next party. Please? Pretty please? I promise we won't yuck up the house."

Danny was only half listening. He was busy wiping butter from the counter. And worrying about the popcorn. Danny liked to keep the house very clean.

"Okay, okay," he said to Michelle. "For your next party."

"Yay!" Michelle cheered.

"Hey, that's cool, kiddo," Uncle Jesse said. He held out his hand. Michelle slapped him "five."

She filled a small bowl with buttery popcorn. Then she ran upstairs to use the phone.

Michelle was excited. A sleepover party! She flopped down on the rug and dialed the phone. She called Cassie Wilkins. Cassie was her best friend.

"Guess what?" Michelle said to Cassie. "I'm going to have a sleepover party!"

"Really? When?" Cassie asked.

"Next Friday night," Michelle said. "Can you come?"

"I don't know," Cassie said. "I've never slept over at anyone's house before. Hold on. I'll ask my mom."

Michelle waited. Finally Cassie came back.

"I can come!" Cassie said into the phone.

"Yay!" Michelle said.

"But who are you going to invite? What will we do?" Cassie asked.

"I don't know," Michelle said. She thought for a moment. "You can help me," she said. "Make a list of people to invite. I'm going to go downstairs to watch Stephanie's party."

"What for?" Cassie asked.

"To find out what we should do at my party," Michelle said. "I want my party to be just like hers."

Michelle said good-bye and hung up the phone. Then she crept down the stairs.

This is fun, Michelle thought. It was like being a spy. She had a pencil and paper with her. She sat behind the railing, near the bottom step. No one noticed her.

Michelle watched Stephanie's two best friends, Allie and Darcy. They were having a pillow fight.

Michelle wrote down THINGS TO DO. Then she wrote PILLOW FIGHT.

Just then, a couch cushion sailed across the living room. It almost hit a lamp!

Well, maybe not, Michelle thought. She crossed PILLOW FIGHT off the list.

She watched the party some more. Stephanie picked up the phone and ordered pizza. Michelle wrote down ORDER PIZZA.

Stephanie played music tapes. Darcy and Mia taught everyone a new dance. Michelle wrote down PLAY MUSIC. DANCE.

Then Stephanie looked at the popcorn bowl. It was empty. "Let's make some more popcorn!" Stephanie shouted.

All at once, Stephanie's friends rushed into the kitchen. Michelle peeked in through the kitchen door. They were making popcorn—all by themselves.

Michelle wrote down MAKE POPCORN—ALL BY MYSELF.

I'm going to do everything just like Stephanie, Michelle thought. Everything! And it's going to be the best sleepover party in the whole world!

Chapter

2

♥ On Monday Michelle went to school. During lunch she told Cassie about her plans.

"We are going to have pizza. And popcorn. And play games," Michelle said.

"That sounds like fun," Cassie said.

"And we can stay up all night!" Michelle said.

"No bedtime?" Cassie asked.

"None," Michelle said.

"Why not? Why don't you have a bedtime?" another girl asked. It was Erin Davis. She was eating lunch at Michelle's table. Her desk was right in front of Michelle's in class. She had curly red hair.

"Because I'm having a sleepover party," Michelle said. "This Friday night. I'll give out the invitations soon. We can stay up all night."

"A sleepover party?" Sarah said loudly. Sarah was also a third grader. She always wore barrettes in her short blond hair.

"Who is having a party?" Mary Beth Alonzo asked. Mary Beth was in Michelle's class, too. She lived two blocks from Michelle's house.

"I am!" Michelle said proudly.

Pretty soon, everyone at the table knew about the party. Michelle felt grown-up. It was fun to plan a party with all her friends.

All day, Michelle talked about the party

with her friends. Everyone had good ideas about what to do.

Cassie wanted to have a dance contest. Sarah said they should bake cookies. And Erin wanted to build a huge tent in the living room—out of furniture.

"That's what my brother always does at his parties," Erin said. "He pushes lots of tables together and drapes blankets over them. Then he makes tunnels by lining up rows of chairs. He drapes sheets over the chairs."

"That's a dumb idea," Sarah said. "It sounds babyish."

"No, it isn't," Erin said. "It's fun. I love tents."

Michelle didn't care about tents that much. She just wanted to have a lot of friends at her party. That was the fun part!

After school, Michelle waited and waited for her father to come home. Finally he walked in the front door.

"Hi, Dad," Michelle said. "Guess what?"

"What?" Danny asked.

"I've got my whole party all planned."

"What party?" Danny asked.

"My sleepover party!" Michelle said.

"Oh," Danny said. "Good for you, Michelle. I'm glad you're planning ahead."

"Right," Michelle said. "Because the party is in only four days."

"What?"

"It's on Friday, Dad," Michelle said.

"Wait a minute, Michelle," Danny said. "You can't have a party without asking me first. And you definitely can't have one this Friday. I haven't gotten over Stephanie's party yet!"

"But, Dad, I did ask you. Remember?" Michelle said. "I asked you last Friday. At Stephanie's party. And you said I could have a sleepover for my next party."

Danny smiled. "Oh, right. But I meant for your next *birthday* party, Michelle. Your birthday is almost a year away!"

"I don't want to wait until my birthday," Michelle said. "I want to have a sleepover party now."

"I'm sorry," Danny said, "but I think you are too young for a sleepover party. The answer is no. You can't have a party this Friday night—and that's final!"

Chapter

3

♥ "I am not too young to have a sleepover party," Michelle said.

"Let's talk about it later," Danny said. He was already on his way to the kitchen.

Michelle started to follow him. But just then, Stephanie came downstairs.

"Too young for what?" Stephanie asked.

"For a slumber party," Michelle said.

"Ha!" Stephanie said. "Yes, you are. You'll never be able to handle it. You'll fall asleep by eleven o'clock."

"No, I won't," Michelle said. "I'll stay up until midnight—just like you did. And then in the morning I'll do what you always do, Stephanie."

"What's that?"

"I'll be cranky and ruin everyone's breakfast," Michelle said.

"Very funny," Stephanie said. "But first you're going to have to talk Dad into letting you have the party."

Right, Michelle thought. But how?

"Michelle. Stephanie. It's time for dinner," Danny called from the kitchen.

Okay, Michelle thought. Now is my chance. I'll show everyone how grown-up I am.

Michelle held her head high in the air. She walked to the kitchen table and sat down. She folded her hands nicely in her lap. See? Michelle thought. This is really grown-up.

Soon Stephanie and D.J. came to the table, too. But they talked and laughed loudly. Stephanie grabbed a glass of milk and started drinking it. D.J. started eating a piece of bread.

Michelle waited for everyone to sit down. She put her napkin on her lap. I'm being polite and they're not, she thought. So there.

"You should act more grown-up," Michelle said to her sisters. "You should wait for everyone to be seated before you start to eat or drink."

"In *this* house?" Stephanie said. "Are you crazy? We'd all starve!"

"Besides," D.J. said, "everyone *is* seated."

"No, they're not," Michelle said. "Aunt Becky, Uncle Jesse, and the twins aren't here."

"That's because they aren't eating with us tonight," D.J. explained. "They went out for pizza earlier."

I don't care, Michelle thought. I'm still acting more grown-up than you.

Danny and Joey served the spaghetti. Spaghetti was one of Michelle's favorite foods. But it was very messy to eat.

Uh-oh, Michelle thought. This was going to be hard.

Joey put a plate in front of Michelle. "Do you want me to cut up your spaghetti for you?" Joey asked.

"No, thank you," Michelle said. "I'm too *grown-up* for that. I'll just eat it the way you do."

"Oh, don't do that," Joey said.

"Why not?" Michelle asked.

"Because I always get it all over my shirt!" Joey replied. Everyone laughed.

Michelle looked at her spaghetti. She put her fork in the middle and started twisting. The spaghetti went around and around her fork. Pretty soon, there was a gigantic blob twisted around her fork. It was enough spaghetti to fill a cereal bowl.

She tried to take a bite. But the blob was too big. It wouldn't fit in her mouth.

"Michelle," Danny said with a laugh, "it looks to me like your eyes are bigger than your stomach."

"Really?" Michelle said seriously. "So *that's* why I can't eat all of this! I didn't know my stomach was so small!"

After dinner Michelle jumped up.

"I'll do the dishes," she said. "After all, I'm *old enough* to help out around here. Aren't I, Dad?"

"Uh, sure," Danny said. "Thank you, Michelle. And Stephanie thanks you, too. It was her night to do the dishes."

Michelle smiled proudly. She cleared the dishes from the table. Then she put them in the dishwasher.

Michelle washed and dried her hands. "I

think I'll just go in the living room," she said. "I haven't read the newspaper yet today."

"The newspaper?" Danny said.

"Yes," Michelle said. "Now that I'm *growing up,* I want to learn about the news."

In the living room, Michelle found the twins playing with toys.

"Hi, Nicky. Hi, Alex," Michelle said.

"Read us a story!" the twins both cried.

"I can't," Michelle said. "I have to read the newspaper."

"Read us a story from the newspaper," Nicky begged.

"Okay," Michelle said. "Come sit down."

Nicky and Alex climbed onto the sofa. Michelle sat between them. She liked to read to the twins, just like their mother Becky did.

Michelle picked up the newspaper. "Stock Prices Fall," Michelle read, looking at a headline.

"Oh, no!" Nicky cried. "Did they get hurt?"

"I don't know," Michelle said. "Let's try another story."

She turned the page. "The President Flies to France," Michelle read.

"The president flies?" Nicky said. "Is he like Superman?"

"No, I think he's more like Clark Kent," Michelle said. "You can tell because they both wear a suit."

"Read us a *real* story!" Alex whined. "I want a real story!"

"Me too!" Nicky cried.

"Okay," Michelle said. "Now, pick out a book you'd like to read."

The twins jumped up and ran over to the bookshelf. They began taking out their picture books. First one, then another. Soon all the books were scattered all over the floor. But they found their favorite book. It was about teddy bears.

Michelle read the book to them twice—once for each twin. Then she sent them upstairs to bed.

Suddenly Michelle noticed that her dad was standing behind her. He had been watching her the whole time.

"Michelle," Danny said, "that was very sweet of you to read to the twins. And very grown-up."

"Really?" Michelle said. Her eyes lit up.

"Yes," Danny said. "And I can see that you are trying to show me how grown-up you are."

Michelle clasped her hands together. "I can be even more grown-up than that," Michelle said. "Watch me!" She got up and put all the twins' books back on the bookshelf.

Danny sat down on the couch and patted the spot next to him. "That's very grown-up, Michelle. Thank you. Now come sit down."

Michelle came and sat beside him.

"Listen, Michelle," Danny said. "I know you really want to have a sleepover party. But I still think you are too young. Your friends might be afraid to sleep here."

"They won't be afraid," Michelle said. "I know because I already asked them."

Danny sighed. "Okay, how about this," he said. "What if you invite just one friend to sleep over on Friday? Like Cassie, for instance."

"No way," Michelle said. "That isn't a slumber party. And you *promised* I could have a slumber party! Now you're going back on your word."

Danny sighed again. He tilted his head

to the left. Then he tilted it to the right. He looked at Michelle sideways. He looked like he was about to give in.

"Please, Dad," Michelle said. "I really am growing up. How about if I alphabetize all the books on the bookshelf?"

Danny laughed.

"I could even alphabetize all my stuffed animals," Michelle said. "Andy the aardvark, Brownie the bear . . ."

"Michelle, you have a stuffed aardvark?" Danny asked.

"Well, no," Michelle said. "I just needed something that began with A."

Danny laughed again.

"Please, Daddy," Michelle said. "Pretty please? Can I have a party?"

"Okay, okay," Danny said. "You win. You can have a small slumber party. But it must be small, Michelle. You may invite only four friends."

"Hooray!" Michelle yelled, jumping up. "Thank you, Daddy. Thank you!"

She threw her arms around Danny's neck and gave him a hug. Then she ran up the stairs to her bedroom. She shared the room with Stephanie.

"I'm going to have a sleepover party!" Michelle announced to Stephanie.

"Thanks for warning me," Stephanie said.

"Why?" Michelle asked.

"Sleepover parties are such a mess," Stephanie said. "I'll probably get stuck cleaning the house for days. I think I'll leave town!"

Chapter 4

♥ Later that night, Michelle flopped down on her bed. She was trying to decide who to invite to her party. She stared at the ceiling for a while. Then she turned over. She let her head hang off the end of the bed. She stared at the floor.

Just then D.J. walked in.

"What's wrong?" D.J. asked.

"I'm having a sleepover party," Michelle explained. "But I can't decide who to invite."

"That's easy," D.J. said. "Just call up

your best friend. Ask *her* to help you plan the party. That way, if it doesn't work out, you'll have someone else to blame."

"Good idea," Michelle said.

"Oh, uh, Michelle," D.J. said. "When is this party, by the way?"

"Friday night. Why?"

"I just wanted to know," D.J. said.

"Why?"

"Because sleepover parties are always such a mess," D.J. said with a laugh. "This way I can be sure to be somewhere else!" Then she left.

Michelle called Cassie, her best friend. She told Cassie that she could invite only four friends. Of course Cassie would be one of them. But who else?

"Let's each make a list," Cassie said. "I'll write down the three people I like best—besides you. And you do the same thing. Then we'll compare our lists."

"Okay," Michelle said. "Hold on."

Michelle got a pencil and paper. She wrote down Erin Davis, Laura Matthews, and Bree Wildau. Then she read the names to Cassie.

"Don't tell me you put Bree on the list," Cassie said. "I don't like her at all. She's too nosy. She always asks me what I brought for lunch—every single day."

"That's what I like about her," Michelle said. "I'm going to invite her. And Erin. And Laura. Who do you have on your list?"

"I have Erin, Laura, and Natalie Cole," Cassie said.

"Who is Natalie Cole?" Michelle asked.

"She's a famous singer," Cassie said. "I like her songs."

"So what?" Michelle said.

"So I'd like to invite her to your party!" Cassie said.

"Forget about Natalie Cole," Michelle said. "Pick someone we know."

"How about Mary Beth Alonzo?" Cassie said.

"No," Michelle said. "She whines too much. She never likes the games we play at recess."

"Well, how about Lindsay Merchison?" Cassie said.

"She's too bossy," Michelle said. "She told me where to sit on the bus when our class went to the zoo."

"Well, it's your party. You decide," Cassie said.

"I'm going to invite Bree Wildau," Michelle said.

"Okay," Cassie said. Then Cassie had to hang up.

Michelle got out her colored markers and paper and sat at her desk. Just then her father came into her room.

"What are you making?" Danny asked.

"Party invitations," Michelle said happily.

"Only four of them, I hope," Danny said.

"Only three," Michelle said. "Because Cassie already knows that she is invited. And she already said she can come."

Michelle drew pictures on the invitations. Pictures of sleeping bags!

One invitation was for Erin. One was for Laura. And one was for Bree. She could hardly wait to pass them out!

The next day Michelle went to school early. She gave the invitations to her friends.

But at lunchtime, Erin came up to Michelle.

"Thanks for the party invitation," Erin said. "But I can't come to your sleepover party."

"Why not?" Michelle asked.

Erin looked at the ground. "Well ..." she said slowly. "I've never slept overnight at someone else's house. I'm used to my own bed. In my own room."

"You can bring your stuffed animals, if you want," Michelle said.

"Can I bring my mom?" Erin asked.

Michelle thought about it. Stephanie's friends never brought *their* mothers to her sleepover parties.

"No," Michelle said.

"Then I can't come," Erin said. "But you can come sleep over at *my* house sometime."

"Thanks," Michelle said.

A few minutes later Laura Matthews came up to Michelle. She said she was glad that Michelle had invited her to the party. And she would love to have Michelle spend the night at *her* house. But she was not ready to sleep at someone else's house. Not yet.

"I get scared of the dark," Laura explained to Michelle.

"Don't worry," Michelle said. "It won't be dark. We aren't going to go to sleep."

"I get tired really early," Laura said. "I can't come."

"Okay," Michelle said sadly.

Now what? She would have to invite two more friends.

Just then, Bree Wildau came up to Michelle.

"I can't come to your party, either," Bree said.

Michelle covered her face with her hands. "Why not?" she asked without even looking at Bree.

"My parents are going away for the weekend. We leave on Friday. Sorry," Bree said.

Now I need *three* more guests! Michelle

thought. Maybe Natalie Cole isn't such a bad idea after all!

Michelle hurried to sit with Cassie. Whispering, she told Cassie all about the party problems.

"How about inviting Amanda Braun?" Cassie suggested.

Michelle looked at Amanda. She was not in Michelle's class this year. But she was wearing a pink and blue skirt. Pink and blue were Michelle's favorite colors.

"Okay," Michelle said.

Michelle walked over to Amanda. Amanda was eating her lunch at another table in the cafeteria with her friends.

Michelle leaned in close to Amanda's ear. She didn't want anyone else to hear her. She didn't want to hurt anyone's feelings.

"I'm having a sleepover party on Friday," Michelle whispered. "Can you come?"

"No," Amanda said out loud.

"Shhhh!" Michelle said. "It's a secret."

"I don't care," Amanda said. "Why didn't you invite me in the first place?"

Michelle blushed. "Because I could only invite four friends," she explained.

"Well, you didn't choose me first," Amanda said. "So I don't want to come now."

Oh, great, Michelle thought. Maybe I should just forget about the whole thing.

By the time school was over, Michelle had invited eight other people to her party. Finally three of them said yes—as long as their parents would say yes. One was Mary Beth Alonzo, the girl who whined. The other was Lindsay Merchison. She was bossy. And the third was Sarah Berger. She was wild sometimes.

Michelle gave Cassie a worried look. "My *best* friends can't come—except for you," Michelle said.

"I know," Cassie said. "And now you're stuck with three girls. One is bossy. One is a whiner. And one is wild."

"Well, I hope they all can come. Do you think it's going to be a good party?" Michelle asked.

Cassie twisted her mouth into a funny shape. "I don't know," she said. "We'll just have to wait till Friday to find out!"

Chapter 5

♥ Michelle was excited about her party. Mary Beth, Lindsay, and Sarah had all gotten permission from their parents. And now Michelle could hardly wait.

"I need someone to make a treasure hunt for my party," Michelle announced at dinner on Thursday night. "Just like at Stephanie's party."

"Oh, Michelle," Danny said. "I'm sorry to tell you this, but I have bad news. I can't help with the treasure hunt. I have to go away on a business trip Friday. But don't worry. There will be lots of other people here to help out."

"I don't need help with anything," Michelle insisted. "Except the treasure hunt."

"I'll help with the treasure hunt," Joey offered. "What do you want me to do?"

"Just hide the treasures Friday," Michelle said. "I'll do everything else."

Finally it was the day of the party. Michelle was so excited, she spilled her orange juice at breakfast. Then she spilled her chocolate milk at lunch. When she got home after school she spilled her apple juice. Joey saw that her shorts were dotted with stains.

"Calm down, Michelle," Joey said. "You already look like you've been in a food fight. And the party hasn't even started yet!"

Michelle glanced at the clock. It was only three-thirty. The party didn't start until five.

"I can't wait!" Michelle said. She ran upstairs and changed her shorts. Then she ran back down to the living room and peeked out the window. No one was at the front door. Of course not! It was only three thirty-five.

For the next hour, Michelle paced back and forth. She fluffed up the sofa pillows. She watched out the window to see if anyone had come yet. She checked over her lists of party plans.

At four-thirty Stephanie and D.J. came downstairs.

"We're out of here," Stephanie announced. "Have fun."

"Where are you going?" Michelle asked.

"Out! Away from the mess!" D.J. said with a laugh. Then she patted Michelle on the head. "But I'm sure you'll have fun, kiddo," she added. "I just don't want to be here to watch the house being destroyed."

"And don't forget what I said," Stephanie added. "You'll be asleep by eleven. I'm betting on it! When I come home later, I'll find all of you sound asleep." Then she and D.J. walked out the front door.

I'm glad they're gone, Michelle thought. Now I can have the whole house to myself. Almost. Joey, Jesse, Becky, and the twins were still home.

From four-thirty until five Michelle sat by the front door. She peeked out the window the whole time.

Finally someone came up the path. It was Cassie. Michelle opened the door.

"Hi!" Cassie said. She carried her sleeping bag into the living room. She put it under a table.

"I'm so glad you're here!" Michelle said. "Now the party has really started."

Soon the doorbell rang again. It was Mary Beth. She stood in the doorway with her arms full. She was carrying a big rolled-up sleeping bag. And a duffel bag of clothes. And two stuffed animals.

"Hmmph!" Mary Beth said from behind her things. But Michelle knew that she was trying to say "hi." Her mouth was just too full of stuffed animals to talk.

"Hi," Michelle said. "Come on in."

Mary Beth marched into the living room and looked around. She dropped her sleeping bag in a chair and let out a big sigh.

Soon Lindsay and Sarah arrived. They put their sleeping bags, pillows, and duffels in a corner.

"What do we do now?" Mary Beth asked in a whiny voice.

"Let's play a game!" Sarah yelled at the top of her lungs.

"Hide-and-seek," Michelle announced. "I'll be it."

"Okay," everyone said.

Michelle closed her eyes tight. She started counting to fifty. She didn't peek—but she listened. She could hear her friends giggling and whispering and running up the stairs.

There are so many places to hide in this house, Michelle thought. But I know all the good places. I bet someone will go all the way up to the attic.

"Forty-eight . . . forty-nine . . . fifty!" Michelle called out. "Ready or not, here I come!"

She opened her eyes and looked around. The living room was empty. Michelle calmly walked up the stairs. She looked in her bedroom, but no one was there.

"Home free!" a voice called out from downstairs. Then another voice called, "Me too. Home free!"

Uh-oh, Michelle thought. Now there were only two people left to find. She looked under D.J.'s bed. No one was hiding there.

"Home free!" a third voice called out from the living room.

No fair, Michelle thought. She was sure that at least *one* of her friends would hide upstairs.

Michelle climbed the steep stairs to the attic. That's where Jesse, Becky, and the twins lived. Michelle heard someone's voice, so she walked on tiptoes. She wanted to sneak up on whoever it was— and tag them really fast.

But when Michelle stepped into the room, she was surprised. Sarah was just sitting on the floor, playing with the twins. She wasn't hiding at all!

Michelle rushed over and tapped Sarah on the arm. "Tag—you're it," Michelle said.

"I'm not hiding," Sarah said. "I'm playing with Nicky and Alex. They are *so* cute! Can we take them downstairs and baby-sit them for a while?"

Michelle looked at Becky.

"It's okay with me," Becky said.

"Okay," Michelle said glumly.

They all went downstairs. Michelle's party was not going exactly as she had planned. But at least everyone was having fun.

For the next half hour Michelle's friends played games with Nicky and Alex. Lindsay read stories to them. And Mary Beth tried to teach them how to count to ten.

Soon, it was time for dinner. Everyone was hungry. Especially the twins.

"In a few minutes I'm going to make noodles for Nicky and Alex," Becky said.

"I'm hungry, too," Lindsay said.

"Do you want me to order pizza for you?" Becky asked Michelle.

"No, thanks," Michelle said. "I'll order it myself." Just like Stephanie did, she thought.

"Okay," Becky said. "But let me know if you need help."

Michelle went to the kitchen to use the phone. The phone number for the pizza place was written on a shiny white board beside the wall phone. Michelle called the pizza place and told them what she wanted.

"Two large plain cheese pizzas," Michelle said. "And please don't put too much tomato sauce on it. We don't like it saucy." Then she hung up.

She hurried back into the living room.

"While we wait for the pizza, let's have a treasure hunt," Michelle suggested.

"Yay!" Sarah screamed. "I love treasure hunts."

"Me too," her other friends agreed.

"This is going to be the best thing we've done all night!" Sarah screamed.

"Wait right here," Michelle said. "I have to go get Joey. He's going to hide the treasures for us."

Michelle went upstairs to Joey's room. She told him that it was time to hide the treasures.

"Fine," Joey said. "But where are they?"

"Where are what?" Michelle asked.

"The treasures. The prizes. The stuff you want me to hide," Joey said.

"Oh, no!" Michelle said. "I forgot all about that part!"

Chapter
6

The Super-Duper Slumber Party

 "You forgot to get the prizes for the treasure hunt?" Joey asked.

Michelle nodded.

"Well, then we can't have a treasure hunt," Joey said.

"Oh, no," Michelle said. Her eyes filled up with tears. "Didn't *you* get the prizes?" she asked Joey.

Joey shook his head. "You told everyone you wanted to plan the party yourself. So I thought you would take care of it."

Michelle's face turned red. Joey was right. She had told everyone that she didn't want any help. Now her treasure hunt was ruined. Maybe it wasn't so easy to plan a party after all.

Michelle swallowed hard. She pushed the tears away. "But if we don't have a treasure hunt," Michelle said, "my friends will be mad at me."

"I'll tell you what," Joey said. "I'll see if I can come up with some prizes myself. Just give me a few minutes."

"Thanks, Joey," Michelle said. She let out a sigh of relief. It was nice to have help. Michelle went back downstairs.

"I'm hungry," Mary Beth whined. "When will the pizza get here?"

Michelle looked at the clock. She could not remember what time it was when she ordered the pizza.

"Soon," Michelle said. "Hey—I have an

idea. Let's play music and dance while we're waiting."

For the next ten minutes Michelle and her friends danced. It was just like Stephanie's party. Then Joey came downstairs with his prizes for the treasure hunt. He showed them to Michelle. The prizes were five balloon animals. He told all the girls to wait in the kitchen while he hid them.

The girls found four of the balloon animals right away. But they couldn't find the fifth one. Soon everyone began to get cranky.

"I'm hungry, hungry, hungry," Sarah said as she jumped up and down on the couch.

"Me too!" Mary Beth whined.

"Me three!" Cassie said. "Why isn't the pizza here yet?"

"I don't know," Michelle said. What would Stephanie do now? she wondered.

And then she remembered. Popcorn! It was on the THINGS TO DO list. Stephanie made microwave popcorn at her party— all by herself. Michelle could do that too!

"I'm going to make popcorn," Michelle said proudly. "We can eat that until the pizza comes. I'll be right back."

Michelle skipped into the kitchen. She climbed on a stool and opened a cabinet. The popcorn was on the top shelf, so she stood on the counter. It was hard to get at. But she didn't want to ask anyone for help. She knew her dad wouldn't want her cooking all by herself in the kitchen. But she had to prove that she was old enough to do it.

"Michelle?" a voice said behind her. It was Jesse. "What are you doing?" he asked. "Do you need some help?"

"I'm going to make popcorn all by myself," Michelle said. "So go away. Okay?"

"Do you know how?" Jesse asked.

"I'll read the instructions on the package," Michelle said, sounding very sure of herself.

"Okay," Jesse said with a shrug. "Call me if you need any help."

Michelle took out the popcorn and opened the clear wrapper. She read the directions carefully. Then she climbed down from the counter to the stool. She jumped to the floor.

"Cook on HIGH for five minutes," Michelle said.

She put the package in the microwave and pushed "5." Nothing happened.

Maybe it needs some zeros, Michelle thought. The numbers on her digital clock always had zeros. She pushed zero. Nothing happened. She stared at the buttons on the microwave. Then she pushed START.

Bingo! The light in the microwave came on. It started to hum. The popcorn was cooking!

Michelle ran back into the living room. "Hey, guess what?" she announced. "The popcorn will be ready in five minutes."

"I'm hungry," Mary Beth whined.

"Let's find the other balloon animal," Michelle said. "Whoever finds it first gets the buttery popcorn on top."

Finally Lindsay found the balloon monkey. It was stuffed into her rolled-up sleeping bag.

"Hooray!" Joey cheered. "You found it!"

Just then Becky came downstairs. She sniffed the air.

"What's that smell?" Becky asked.

"What smell?" Joey said.

"Coming from the kitchen," Becky said.

"It must be the popcorn," Michelle said. "Maybe it's done."

Michelle and Becky ran into the kitchen. Smoke was pouring out of the microwave oven.

"Oh, no!" Michelle yelled. "It's on fire!"

Chapter

7

♥ "Fire?" Joey shouted. He rushed into the kitchen. Becky ran to the microwave. She pushed the STOP button to turn it off. Then she yanked open the door.

Inside, the bag of popcorn was in flames.

'Oh, no, Michelle thought. Fire! The flames were so scary. Was the kitchen going to burn down? If it did, it would be Michelle's fault.

And then she thought, things like this never happened at Stephanie's party.

Quickly Joey ran to the sink. He filled a glass with water and ran back to the microwave. He threw the water into the oven to put out the flames.

The water splashed back out. It started to drip on the floor. But at least the popcorn bag stopped burning.

"Boy, Michelle," Joey said. "I'd say your party is getting pretty *hot!*"

Becky put her hands on her hips. "How did this happen?" Becky asked Michelle.

Michelle shrugged. "Too many microwaves?" she said.

"No," Becky said, shaking her head. "Too many *minutes.* When I came in here, I looked at the microwave. It was counting down from thirty-eight minutes. How long did you set it for?"

"I pushed five—and then I pushed zero to make it five minutes," Michelle said.

Becky and Joey rolled their eyes. "Michelle," Joey said, "that means you pushed fifty. Fifty minutes. No wonder the bag caught on fire."

"I'm sorry," Michelle said. "But everyone was hungry. And the pizza didn't come. So I thought I'd make popcorn as a snack."

"I'll call the pizza place to find out what happened," Becky offered. "But next time you want to cook something, promise me you'll get an adult to help."

"Okay," Michelle said in a very small voice. She felt like a little kid who couldn't do anything right.

Becky picked up the phone. She dialed the pizza place.

"Hello? This is Becky at the Tanner house," Becky said. "About an hour ago, we ordered some pizza. It still hasn't come."

Becky talked on the phone for a minute.

Then she covered the mouthpiece of the phone with her hand. "Michelle, did you forget to give your name and address?" Becky asked.

"Whoops," Michelle said.

Becky took her hand away from the phone and talked again. "Uh, I think we did forget to give an address. Uh-huh. No phone number, either. I'm sorry about that," Becky said.

Quickly Becky told the man where to bring the pizza. Then she hung up.

"Sorry," Michelle said. "I guess I should have asked for help."

"That's right," Becky said. She put her arm around Michelle. "But I'm proud of you for *trying* to do so many things by yourself."

Michelle smiled. Becky was nice.

"Maybe we'd better go see how your friends are doing," Becky said. "It's getting pretty noisy in the living room."

"Okay," Michelle said.

She hurried into the living room. Shrieks and screams filled the air. When Michelle got there, she saw why.

Sarah was jumping up and down on the couch, doing gymnastics. She screamed a little bit each time she bounced. Beside her, Lindsay was pretending to be Sarah's coach. She shouted orders at Sarah.

"Jump higher!" Lindsay yelled. "Do a flip!"

"Watch this!" Sarah shouted. She twisted in the air and landed on her feet.

"Let's go play a board game in my room," Michelle said.

Before Michelle finished, Sarah jumped off the couch. She raced up the stairs, taking them two at a time. Lindsay followed right behind her. Michelle had to hurry to catch up with them.

By the time Michelle got to her room, Sarah was already pulling toys and stuffed animals off the shelves.

"Wait," Michelle said. "Don't take everything down at once." Michelle shared the room with Stephanie. She didn't want Stephanie to see a big mess in the room.

But Sarah ignored her. "What's in here?" she asked. She opened Michelle's closet door and started looking around. "Hey—can I try on your sister's boots?"

"Not unless you ask her," Michelle tried to say. But it was too late. Sarah had already stepped into a pair of red and black cowboy boots. Then she poked her head into the back of the closet and pulled out some old dolls.

"Let's have a tea party!" Sarah yelled. "Let's get out all your old dolls. We can bring them downstairs and have a tea party!"

"No—let's have a sleepover party for the dolls!" Lindsay said in an even louder voice.

"No, a tea party!" Sarah insisted. She yanked more dolls out of the closet.

Michelle felt like a tornado was sweeping through her room. All her dolls, her clothes, her toys, and her games were being pulled out at once. Within a few minutes the room was a mess.

"Stop it," Michelle tried to say. But no one listened.

Just then Becky called from downstairs. "Pizza is here!"

Sarah dropped everything she was carrying on the floor. She kicked off the cowboy boots. Then she ran downstairs.

"I'm starved," Lindsay said, running right behind her.

Michelle looked at the mess on the floor. She wanted to clean it up, but her stomach was growling. She was starving, too.

Slowly Michelle walked down the stairs to the kitchen. The pizza boxes were sitting on the table. Michelle's friends were pushing and fighting about where to sit.

This is no fun, Michelle thought. She didn't like it when people pushed. Or when they were wild.

Mary Beth opened the top box and grabbed a slice of pizza. She took a bite.

"Oh, no!" she said. "It's cold!"

Right then, Comet the dog came bounding into the room. He jumped up on the table.

"Stay down, Comet!" Michelle yelled. But it was too late. His front paws landed on top of a pizza box. It was sticking out over the edge of the table. An instant later the pizza fell face down on the floor with a splat!

Michelle felt a lump forming in her throat. I wish I never had this stupid party in the first place! she thought.

Chapter
8

♥ For a minute Comet sniffed at the pizza on the floor.

"Yuck," Sarah said. "I don't want to eat that pizza *now*. It's all doggie."

Michelle picked the pizza box up. The pizza was squished to the lid. What a mess! Michelle thought. She didn't want to eat it, either.

"Well, we can still eat the other one," Michelle said.

Sarah picked up a piece of pizza from

the other box. She took one bite and made a face. "Yuck!" she said. "I *hate* cold pizza. And it's too saucy."

"I know," Mary Beth agreed. "The sauce is gooshing out all over the place."

Michelle gave Cassie a pleading look. Her face said, Help!

Cassie understood. "Well, I think the pizza is good," Cassie said. "Maybe we just need to warm it up in the micro—"

"NO!" Michelle said. "No more microwave."

"Okay," Cassie said glumly. She forced herself to take another bite.

Sarah jumped up from the table. "Let's see what else you have to eat around here," she said.

She marched over to the kitchen counter and climbed up on it. Then she pulled open a cabinet door. "Hey—candy!" she announced.

Michelle shook her head. "I don't think we're allowed to eat candy before dinner," she started to say.

But it was too late. Sarah had already grabbed a bag of M&M's. She was eating them by the handful.

Mary Beth leaned over to whisper in Michelle's ear. "Watch out," she warned. "Sarah gets wild when she gets hold of candy."

Gets wild? Michelle thought. It seemed like Sarah was pretty wild already!

"Let's get into our sleeping bags," Cassie said. "Then maybe we can watch a movie."

"Or tell ghost stories," Sarah shouted.

"Okay—but I get to sleep beside Sarah," Lindsay yelled as she raced into the living room.

Michelle ran to find her sleeping bag. It was in a ball in the corner—not where she had left it at all. Someone had kicked it out of the way while they were jumping on the couch. Quickly Michelle dragged her sleeping bag back toward the couch.

"I want to sleep there," Mary Beth whined.

"No, that's Michelle's place," Cassie said. "It's her house."

"It's not fair," Mary Beth said to Michelle. "You can sleep there anytime you want. I'm the guest. I should get to sleep where I want."

"Wait! Wait! I have an idea!" Lindsay shouted. "I'm thinking of a number from one to ten. Whoever guesses it can sleep on the couch."

"Five!" Mary Beth called out.

"Seven!" Sarah said.

"Two!" Cassie cried.

"Hey—it's *my* party," Michelle tried to say. But no one listened.

"Ha, ha," Lindsay said. "The number was nine. Nobody guessed it. So *I* get to sleep on the couch. And I choose Sarah to sleep next to me."

"Well, I don't care," Mary Beth said. "You can't tell me what to do, Lindsay Merchison. I can sleep on the couch if I want to."

Mary Beth stomped over to the couch and sat down. But Lindsay was already lying there. So she sat right on top of her.

"Get off!" Lindsay said.

"Make me!" Mary Beth said.

TWEEEEEET! Suddenly a loud whistle screamed in Michelle's ears.

She turned around and saw Joey standing in the doorway. He had just come downstairs from his bedroom. He was blowing a whistle. He looked mad.

"Hey—quiet down in here," Joey said. "I think it's time for you girls to go to bed."

"That's what we're trying to do," Michelle said. "But everyone's fighting about where to sleep."

Joey told everyone where to put their sleeping bags. Then he said, "Time for lights out. But you can talk for a while if you want. Quietly."

Joey flipped the lights out and went back upstairs. All of a sudden it was very dark.

"I don't like the dark," Mary Beth said softly.

"Me either," Sarah said. "I have a night light at home."

"My mom leaves the hall light on," Mary Beth said.

"Don't be silly," Lindsay said. Michelle thought she sounded scared, too.

"Let's turn on a light," Mary Beth said.

"No," Michelle said. "If we turn the lights on, everyone will be noisy again."

In the dark she thought about how her party was going. So far, it had been a mess. Her friends had been fighting. She had forgotten to get prizes for the treasure hunt. The popcorn caught on fire. The pizza was cold.

Now Michelle was tired. She yawned and looked at the clock. It was only nine. But Michelle didn't care. She didn't want to stay up until midnight. Not anymore.

"I have to call my mom," Mary Beth said in the dark.

She stood up and stumbled across the living room. She opened the door to the kitchen. A beam of light streamed into the room.

While Mary Beth called her mother, everyone told jokes.

Michelle told her favorite knock-knock joke. Then Cassie told a joke. Pretty soon, everyone felt better.

Mary Beth came back to the living room. "I have to pack up my things," she said. "My mom is coming to get me."

"Really?" Michelle was surprised. She sat up in her sleeping bag. "How come?"

"I don't feel well," Mary Beth said.

Michelle reached over and flipped on a light. She squinted at Mary Beth. Mary Beth had a small smile on her face—like she wasn't really sick. Like she was faking.

Five minutes later Mary Beth's mother rang the doorbell. They only lived a few blocks away.

"Thanks for inviting me to your party," Mary Beth said. "Sorry I have to go." But she had a huge smile on her face. She looked like she was happy to leave.

Michelle felt bad. She didn't want Mary Beth to go home. It made Michelle feel like her party was no fun.

"Do we have to turn the lights off again?" Lindsay asked.

"Yes," Michelle said. "But we can leave the kitchen door open. That way some light will come in."

Michelle got up and opened the kitchen door. Then she climbed back into her sleeping bag. The floor was hard. She twisted and turned. She couldn't get comfy.

"I need a drink," Lindsay announced. "I'll get it myself."

Lindsay got up and put on her slippers. They had big doggie faces on them. She padded to the kitchen in her nightgown. She was gone a long time. Then Michelle heard her talking.

Michelle tiptoed to the kitchen to see what was going on. Lindsay was just hanging up the phone.

"I called my mother," Lindsay explained as she shuffled back to the living room. She had a guilty look on her face. "I think I might feel sick, too. My mom says I should come home."

"I need to go home, too," Sarah said, jumping up. "I don't feel well, either."

Michelle and Cassie looked at each other. They both shrugged. They knew the other girls weren't really sick. They just wanted to go home.

Soon Lindsay and Sarah were gone. Then Joey came upstairs and stuck his head into the living room.

"Hey—what's going on?" he asked. He sounded worried. "It's too quiet down here."

"Everyone went home," Michelle told him.

Michelle felt like she was going to cry. Her party was over. It was a big flop.

Then she turned to Cassie. "Are you going to go home, too?" Michelle asked.

Chapter 9

♥ Big tears began to fill Michelle's eyes. All her friends had left her—except one. Maybe Cassie was going to leave, too!

"No," Cassie said, "I'm not going home. I'm having fun! And anyway, it will be more fun this way," she whispered. "Now we can just be together and talk. Maybe we'll tell ghost stories."

Michelle let out a little sigh. "Thanks," she said. But she still had a huge lump in her throat. She still felt like she might cry.

"Let's go sleep upstairs," Cassie said. "We don't have to sleep in the living room, do we?"

"No," Michelle said. "But my room is a mess."

"That's okay," Cassie said. "I'll help you clean it up."

Joey came over to Michelle and put his arm around her. "Are you okay?" he asked her.

"I guess so," Michelle said.

"Okay," Joey said. "You go clean up your room."

It only took Michelle and Cassie fifteen minutes to get Michelle's room straightened up. Then they spread their sleeping bags out on the floor. Michelle thought about sleeping in her bed, because it would be softer. But she decided not to. She wanted to sleep next to her best friend.

Just as they were about to snuggle down into their sleeping bags, Becky came upstairs. She had a big tray in her arms. On the tray were two plates with grilled cheese sandwiches. And some cookies. And juice.

"I thought you two might still be hungry," Becky said with a warm smile.

"Thanks!" Cassie said, sitting up quickly. "I'm starved."

"Me too," Michelle said. She remembered the cold pizza.

Becky put the tray on the end of Michelle's bed. The girls knelt beside it and used the bed like a table. They ate the sandwiches hungrily.

Then Cassie went to the bathroom to wash her face and brush her teeth.

When she was gone, Michelle looked up at Becky.

"My party was a big flop," Michelle said.

"Oh, I don't think so," Becky said. "Your friends seemed to have fun—until it was time for bed. I just think they are a little too young to sleep at someone else's house. They were just homesick. That's all."

"I know," Michelle said. "Maybe next time I'll have to invite older friends."

Becky laughed.

"Well, you know what?" Becky said. "I think you should wait a while before you have another sleepover party."

"I guess so," Michelle said. "I guess I wouldn't want to sleep at someone else's house, either. Except maybe at Cassie's."

"That's right," Becky said. She gave Michelle a squeeze. "But you know what else? In about a year you'll be old enough for a sleepover party. And then it will be really fun."

"Do you think so?" Michelle asked.

Becky nodded. "I know so," she said. then she added, "You know, Michelle, when you are young it always looks like fun to do grown-up things. But it's not so much fun to do them before you're really ready."

Michelle sighed. "I just wanted my party to be like Stephanie's," she said. "I tried to do everything Stephanie did. But it didn't work out."

"Did someone mention my name?" Michelle looked up and saw Stephanie standing in the doorway.

"Hi," Michelle said.

"Hi," Stephanie said. "How did it go?"

"Not so great," Michelle said.

Stephanie came in and sat down on Michelle's bed. Becky picked up the tray of dishes and carried it out.

"So tell me everything," Stephanie said. "What happened?"

"Everything," Michelle said. "My friends fought with each other about where they would sleep. And made a huge mess. And wouldn't do anything I said. And I started a fire in the microwave. And the pizza was cold."

Stephanie smiled. "Hey—don't feel so bad, Michelle," she said. "My parties don't always go smoothly, either."

"Oh, yes, they do," Michelle said. "I spied on your party. It was perfect."

"That was while you were *awake*," Stephanie said with a laugh. "But after you went to sleep, it was a disaster! My friends fought about where to sleep, too."

"Really?" Michelle asked.

"Uh-huh." Stephanie nodded. "And we tried to make chocolate fudge. But it burned. I ruined one of Dad's pans."

"Really?"

"Uh-huh," Stephanie said.

"But at least your friends didn't get scared and go home at ten o'clock," Michelle said.

"That's true," Stephanie agreed. "That's because we're older."

Michelle nodded. "Anyway, it's more fun to have just Cassie spend the night," Michelle said. "We're going to stay up late. And tell each other ghost stories."

"Oh, really?" Stephanie said. One of her eyebrows went up. She stared at the floor behind Michelle.

Michelle turned around to see what her sister was looking at. There was Cassie—asleep in her sleeping bag!

"I thought she was brushing her teeth!" Michelle said. "I didn't even hear her come back in."

Stephanie laughed. "Oh, well," she said. "I told you you'd be asleep by eleven!"

Michelle pouted. She felt grumpy again. Stephanie gave her a hug.

"Come on," Stephanie said. "Let's go downstairs and have a snack. *I'll* tell you a ghost story."

"I already had a snack," Michelle said. "But I could use some more juice."

The two sisters walked down to the kitchen. All the lights in the living room were off.

"Sit on the couch," Stephanie said in a spooky voice. "I'll bring the juice in here."

Michelle giggled. This was fun. She loved the ghost stories that Stephanie told. They were never *too* scary. Just scary enough.

Stephanie came back with a big glass of grape juice.

"Here—" she said. "Drink this. It's bat's blood!"

Michelle giggled again.

"Now," Stephanie said in a scary voice,

"I'll tell you how we happened to have bat's blood in our refrigerator!"

For the next five minutes Stephanie told Michelle the ghost story. It was a long funny story about vampires and skeletons and bats. And about how Joey was trying to start a baseball team, but he got confused. He bought real-live bats instead of baseball bats! Michelle giggled the whole time.

"Okay," Stephanie said when she was finished. "I'm tired. It's time for bed."

Michelle got up to go to bed. She stepped on something with her bare foot. She picked her foot up and saw what it was—an orange M&M.

"Wait, Stephanie," Michelle said. "We can't go to bed yet!"

"Why not?" Stephanie said, yawning.

"Look at this mess." Michelle pointed to the glasses of juice. And pieces of half-eaten pizza. And smushed M&M's. "What if Dad sees this?"

"You're right, Michelle," Stephanie said. "Dad would—"

Just then someone put a key in the front door. Michelle saw the doorknob turn.

"Oh, no," Michelle whispered. "Is that Dad?"

Chapter 10

♥ Michelle crossed her fingers and held her breath. She didn't want her father to see the mess she and her friends had made. The door opened. Light from the porch streamed into the dark room. Michelle looked up to see who it was.

Whew! It was D.J.! She was just coming home from a date. She flipped a light on—and gasped.

"What a mess!" D.J. said.

"We can't let Dad see this," Michelle said.

"Yeah," Stephanie agreed. "Dad is coming home late tonight. In fact, he'll be here any minute!"

"And he will be really mad if he sees this," D.J. said.

Quickly the three sisters started to tackle the job. Michelle fixed the chair cushions. Stephanie collected the juice glasses. D.J. picked up all the yucky pizza.

Soon Joey, Jesse, and Becky joined in. With everyone working together, the house was clean in no time.

Michelle yawned. She was very tired now. Slowly she climbed the stairs to her room.

Cassie was still asleep on the floor. So Michelle spread her sleeping bag out right next to Cassie. She put it on the floor near the end of her bed.

Then she fluffed up two pillows. She

snuggled down into her sleeping bag and closed her eyes.

"Michelle?" a voice whispered.

Michelle opened her eyes and looked up. Danny was standing in the doorway.

"Dad! You're home," Michelle said sleepily.

"Yup," Danny said. "And I just wanted to come upstairs and tell you how proud I am of you."

He bent down to give Michelle a hug.

"What for?" Michelle said.

"Well," Danny said. "I walked in the door and took one look around the house. It's perfectly clean. So I realized something. You decided not to have a sleepover party after all."

"Uh, Dad," Michelle tried to say. "That's not exactly what happened."

"Sure, it is," Danny said with a yawn. "You just invited Cassie over—like I suggested."

"No, I didn't," Michelle tried to say. But Danny stood up to leave.

"You can tell me about it some other time," he said. "I'm really tired. I just wanted you to know. I'm glad you decided to wait until next year for a sleepover party. That was a very grown-up thing to do!"

Michelle smiled to herself.

Right, she thought. Next year. She would be more grown-up by then. And then she was going to have the best sleepover party in the whole world!

YOU COULD WIN
A VISIT TO THE WARNER BROS. STUDIO!

One First Prize: Trip for up to three people to the Warner Bros.
Studios in Burbank, CA, home of the "Full House" Set

Ten Second Prizes: "Stephanie" posters autographed by
actress Jodi Sweetin

Twenty-Five Third Prizes: One "Full House" Stephanie
Boxed Set

Name_____Birthdate_____

Address_____

City_____State_____Zip_____

Daytime Phone_____

POCKET BOOKS/"Full House" SWEEPSTAKES

Official Rules:

1. No Purchase Necessary. Enter by submitting the completed Official Entry Form (no copies allowed) or by sending on a 3" x 5" card your name, address, daytime telephone number and birthdate to the Pocket Books/"Full House" Sweepstakes, Advertising and Promotion Department, 13th Floor, 1230 Avenue of the Americas, NY, NY 10020. Entries must be received by April 30, 1995. Not responsible for lost, late or misdirected mail. Enter as often as you wish, but one entry per envelope. Winners will be selected at random from all entries received in a drawing to be held on or about May 1, 1995.

2. Prizes: One First Prize: a weekend (3 days/2 nights) for up to three people (the winning minor, his/her parent or legal guardian and one guest) including round-trip coach airfare from the major U.S. airport nearest the winner's residence, ground transportation or car rental, meals and two nights in a hotel (one room, triple occupancy), plus a visit to the Warner Bros. Studios in Burbank, California (approximate retail value: $3,200.00). Winner must be able to travel on the dates designated by sponsor between June 1, 1995 and December 31, 1995. Ten Second Prizes: One "Stephanie" poster autographed by actress Jodi Sweetin (retail value: $15.00) Twenty-Five Third Prizes: One "Full House: Stephanie" Boxed Set (retail value: $14.00).

3. The sweepstakes is open to residents of the U.S. no older than fourteen as of April 30, 1995. Proof of age required to claim prize. Prizes will be awarded to the winner's parent or legal guardian. Void in Puerto Rico and wherever else prohibited by law. Employees of Paramount Communications, Inc., Warner Bros., their suppliers, affiliates, agencies, participating retailers, and their families living in the same household are not eligible. One prize per person or household. Prizes are not transferable and may not be substituted. The odds of winning a prize depend upon the number of entries received.

4. All federal, state and local taxes are the responsibility of the winners. Winners will be notified by mail. Prize winners may be required to execute and return an Affidavit of Eligibility and Release within 15 days of notification or an alternate winner will be selected. Winners grant Pocket Books and Warner Bros. the right to use their names, likenesses, and entries for any advertising, promotion and publicity purposes without further compensation to or permission from the entrants, except where prohibited by law. For a list of major prize winners, (available after May 5, 1995) send a stamped, self-addressed envelope to Prize Winners, Pocket Books/"Full House: Stephanie" Sweepstakes, Advertising and Promotion Department, 13th Floor, 1230 Avenue of the Americas, NY, NY 10020.

FULL HOUSE, characters, names and all related indicia are trademarks of Warner Bros. Television © 1994.

Oct94-01

Join eight-year old Nancy
and her best friends as they
collect clues and solve mysteries in

THE NANCY DREW NOTEBOOKS™

#1: THE SLUMBER PARTY SECRET

#2: THE LOST LOCKET

#3: THE SECRET SANTA

#4: BAD DAY FOR BALLET

#5: THE SOCCER SHOE CLUE

by Carolyn Keene
Illustrated by Anthony Accardo

A MINSTREL® BOOK
Published by Pocket Books

1045-01

FULL HOUSE™

Michelle

#1: THE GREAT PET PROJECT

#2: THE SUPER-DUPER SLEEPOVER PARTY

Based on the Hit TV Series!

Available from

A MINSTREL® BOOK

Published by Pocket Books